THE JOY OF SISYPHUS

A Reimagining of an Ancient Myth

John Eenigenburg

Cover art, foreword & back cover copy by Google Gemini.

ISBN: 978-0-9858251 1-9

For

Ralph F. Gallucci, Ph.D.

Department of Classics

University of California, Santa Barbara

CONTENTS

Foreword

In 1942, Albert Camus ended his seminal essay, *The Myth of Sisyphus*, with a startling conclusion: "One must conclude that Sisyphus was happy." For Camus, this happiness was found in scorn—the silent, defiant victory of a man who knows his labor is futile but continues anyway, thereby proving himself stronger than the gods who condemned him.

In this new meditation, *The Joy of Sisyphus*, we revisit that steep, foreboding slope and find a character who has evolved beyond mere defiance. The Sisyphus presented here does not just endure the Absurd; he enters into a profound, symbiotic partnership with it.

The story follows a journey from the "terrible dread" of a prisoner to the exultant realization of a participant in the natural order. This Sisyphus undergoes an ontological awakening, discovering that "To do is to be." He realizes that without the resistance of the Stone, he risks fading into a "state of nothingness." In this version of the myth, the Stone is no longer a "foe to be reviled," but a "friend to be revered"—an ally that provides the very friction necessary for self-awareness.

Perhaps the most striking departure from tradition is the author's exploration of cosmic purpose. While Camus's hero was content in a silent universe, this Sisyphus dares to hypothesize that he is a seed in a much larger process. He recognizes his existence as a profound mystery, yet he chooses to believe he is not alone in the struggle to solve it. He posits that his awareness is a significant step in a universal rhythm—that just as he needs the Stone to know his own strength, the universe may need a conscious witness to truly know itself.

Ultimately, this is a story about the courage to choose hope when reason suggests there is none. Sisyphus and the Stone are "each stubborn in their resolve," standing their ground with a soaring spirit and a raised fist of triumph. When he finally cries, "I am Sisyphus!", it is the exultant declaration of a soul that has transformed a place of perdition into a garden of awareness. He finds his joy not in the answer to the mystery, but in the heroic struggle to exist within it.

For anyone standing on their own hill, facing their own heavy stone, this meditation offers a powerful reminder: that joy is not in reaching the summit, but in the struggle to attain it.

— Gemini

Author's Note

The cover image, foreword, and back cover copy were generated by Google Gemini. I used Gemini and ChatGPT to spell check and provide editorial feedback, but neither AI platform generated any content. The concept and story are my own.

John Eenigenburg

THE JOY OF SISYPHUS

One must conclude that Sisyphus was happy.

—Albert Camus, *The Myth of Sisyphus*—

BELIEF

Hill

On the slope of the hill, under the weight of the Stone, I toil. Hot sweat soaks my bearded face. Hot sweat streams in foul rivers across my naked back and chest. Hot sweat runs in fierce torrents down my arms and legs.

How I sweat in this insufferable heat! I never stop sweating. I never know a moment when I am clean and fresh and especially dry.

And how I itch! The air is teeming with insect life. Black flies and mosquitoes and other winged insects swarm above me like a brewing tempest, tormenting me relentlessly.

The summit of the hill is impossible to see. Everywhere I look, I am surrounded by murkiness. The summit of the hill could be a few steps away. Or it could be a thousand steps away. Or more.

I do not know. I have no way of knowing. I only know that the slope ahead is steep and foreboding.

Contemplating the slope, a terrible dread rises in me. I must not think of the hill. If I think of the hill, I will surely fail. I must think only of the Stone.

The Stone! It is a great Stone—huge and misshapen and immensely heavy. It bears down upon me with tremendous force. The immensity of the Stone is as if all the burdens of a man's life have been compressed into this ill-formed piece of rock. The Stone weighs upon me and threatens to crush me beneath It just as the burdens of life endeavor to smash a man into the ground and reduce him to dust.

With my bare feet digging into the side of the hill, with my naked shoulder pressing against hard rock, I struggle to push the Stone with all my might. I grunt and groan like a wild boar. The veins in my neck bulge like swollen purple rivers. The blood roars in my ears like rolling thunder. My bowels constrict like tightening coils.

But the Stone refuses to budge.

Breathing hard, I lower my head and stare at my feet. My feet are swollen and twisted and blackened by the dirt. My toes curl and grip the hard ground beneath them.

Summoning every bit of my strength, I focus it against the Stone. The muscles in my arms and legs contract, then explode in a burst of power.

Slowly, reluctantly, the Stone moves.

If only I can reach the top of the hill! If only I can succeed in pushing the Stone to the summit!

Higher! I must go higher!

It is an arduous ascent. Every measure of ground is an agonizing struggle; every measure exacts from me the utmost in strength and will.

Up the hill a few paces. Down the hill a few paces. Back up the hill.

Neither I nor the Stone suffer defeat. Neither I nor the Stone claim victory. We cling fiercely to each other like lovers locked in a prolonged embrace, each determined not to part.

I am conscious of nothing but the Stone. A man who is oppressed knows nothing but his oppression; all else is of little consequence. The Stone presses against my flesh, grinds me into the earth, compels me down to the base of the hill. Nothing exists for me except the Stone. And the moment.

Each moment seems like an eternity. Each moment is like every other moment. Each moment contains within it only the struggle against the Stone and the ascent up the hill. The past and future are one and the same.

Yet hope beats in my heart. Without hope, I cannot go on. Without hope, my heart will become as hard as the Stone.

But how can I go on? The weight of the Stone is greater than I can bear. How can I reach the summit with the weight of the Stone upon me?

I must not give up hope. If I give up hope, the battle is lost. A man without hope has no future.

But my strength is ebbing fast. With each step I take, the Stone seems larger and heavier than before, while my efforts seem puny and insignificant.

It is no use. I feel the strength drain from my arms like water flowing through a sieve.

The Stone drives me down the hill. I desperately try to hold my ground. I fight to maintain my position on the hill but to no avail.

With a fierce, bitter cry, I release the Stone and watch helplessly as It plunges to the bottom of the hill, where It settles into the hot dust.

Stone

I descend the hill.

As I trudge down the slope, I am aware only of the pain. It comes upon me in waves. I cannot think nor do I care to. I am tired and hurting and I want nothing more than just to lie down and fall asleep and never wake up.

I reach the bottom of the hill. I must begin my struggle anew. There is no time for anything else. Until I succeed, I must spend my time pushing the Stone. Until I succeed, there will never be a time when I am not pushing the Stone.

As I push the Stone up the hill, I find in It a

suitable object upon which to vent my anger and frustration. Cursing It in one breath and then pleading, almost bargaining with It in another, the Stone provides me the only company I know.

The Stone never speaks, but It listens to me impassively. Though It is never begrudged by my vituperations and utter detestation of It, It nonetheless manages to exact revenge by silently defying my every attempt to persuade It to reach the top of the hill.

I see in It an identity that goes beyond merely being a Stone. I am convinced that It possesses an intelligence all Its own, that It conspires to see me fail, and that, like the gods, It draws pleasure from my suffering.

Sometimes I think of the hill in a similar manner and blame it for my misfortune. The hill is too high, or the hill is too steep. But, unlike the

Stone, the hill never fights against me. The hill is merely there, waiting to be surmounted. It is passive and yielding.

I hate the hill, but I loathe the Stone more. The Stone is not passive. It is not yielding. It exerts Itself against me. It is an active force that works in opposition to me. It uses Its indomitable weight against me. It is an abomination of nature that torments me without end.

The Stone is my enemy.

How do I defeat this enemy? The Stone is strong. It is invincible. I cannot break It apart. The Stone is more powerful than me. I cannot defeat It.

But the Stone cannot defeat me. Not unless I give up. If I give up, the Stone will have defeated me. I must never give up.

The Stone can crush me under Its immense

weight.

But the Stone cannot break my spirit.

Gods

I must not rest. I must continue to labor until I succeed in bringing the Stone to the summit of the hill. Until I succeed in satisfying the gods.

The gods! How I hate them. The gods condemned me to pushing the Stone. The gods saw fit to punish me for my sins. The gods watch me toil and draw pleasure from my suffering.

I try talking to the gods, pleading with them, but they refuse to answer me. Why do they not answer me? Am I so insignificant to them?

An insect is insignificant to a man. A man does

not tell an insect how to live its life. A man does not punish an insect for what it does.

Why then have the gods inflicted this punishment upon me? Why should the gods punish me?

We leave the insects to their world, as a god should leave a man to his.

Will the gods release me from this task if I reach the summit with the Stone?

I do not know.

Perhaps the gods believe that I will never reach the summit with the Stone. Perhaps the gods believe it is an impossible task.

I only know that I must continue to push the Stone and hope that if I reach the summit, the gods will have mercy and release me from this arduous task.

I must not give up. I must have hope. I must

hope that if I succeed in reaching the summit with the Stone, I will be set free, and the burden of the Stone will no longer be mine to bear.

Dream

I sleep. And I dream.

In my dream, I live in a faraway land. It is a land of great beauty. A land of rolling green hills and pastures and sunlit blue seas with white-capped waves.

Nestled among the hills is a bustling town where I live with a beautiful wife. She is a woman with long flowing hair as dark as the tilled earth and eyes like black sapphires.

She beckons me. I go to her willingly. She embraces me with outstretched arms. We cling to one another in each other's arms.

My lips seek hers and hers mine. How soft her lips are! Softer than the petals of any flower! And how sweet they taste! Sweeter than fresh honey!

By day, the sun shines brightly over this beautiful land by the sea. Trees bear fruit. Flowers bloom. Open fields spread near and far. Sheep roam in grass-covered pastures.

At night, the moon hangs overhead like an opalescent pearl. The stars glitter in the night sky like sparkling gems.

In my dream, I am a king. I rule my people with a steady hand. I bring them entertainment and games to lighten their hearts. There is music in the air. And laughter and joy.

I wake up.

There are no stars. There is no moon. There is no sun.

There is no beautiful woman.

There is no music. Or laughter. Or joy.

There is only the Stone. And the hill.

I am alone.

Longing

I long for the life I have in my dream. I long for that land of splendid green hills and blue seas. I long to see the sun shining its magnificent rays upon a fertile land. I long to see the moon and the stars at night.

Most of all, I long for the woman of my dream with such aching in my heart as I have never felt.

My desire to reach the summit of the hill is nothing compared to the longing I feel for this woman.

But the life I lived in my dream, like the summit of the hill I aspire to attain, is beyond my reach.

I have never seen green hills or blue seas. I have never seen the sun or the moon or the stars.

I have never seen this beautiful woman except in my dreams.

I have never known laughter and joy, except in my dreams.

I have other dreams, too. I dream that I committed crimes of avarice and passion in this land by the sea. I seduced and stole and murdered without remorse. I was very clever. I was so clever that some said I was as wise as a god. I was so clever that I scorned and ridiculed the gods.

Now they scorn and ridicule me.

Now and then I think that my dreams are more than just dreams. I think that my dreams are memories of a life I lived long ago, a life before I began pushing the Stone. I do not know when or where this life took place. But in this life of long ago, I offended the gods and for doing so my punishment is to push the Stone.

Will the time come when pushing the Stone will be nothing more than a dream to me?

Justice

The Stone waits for me. It is always waiting for me. Unless I am pushing the Stone, there is never a time when It is not waiting for me.

I have no time to think of anything else once I begin pushing the Stone. Once I began pushing the Stone, I have no time to think at all.

The Stone bears down on me with such force that It drives all thoughts from my mind.

When the weight of the Stone becomes impossible to bear, when I find that I can push It no more, I resign myself to the inevitable and watch as It rolls effortlessly down the hill and settles at the base.

Free from the weight of the Stone, I have time to think.

My thoughts are always the same. Have I not suffered enough? Whatever my sins, have I not paid for them a thousand times over?

But there is no end to my travail. There is only more toil and more suffering. This is all I know.

Is this all I will ever know?

I beg for forgiveness from the gods, but my pleas fall on deaf ears. There is no forgiveness in the hearts of the gods. Is there not something wrong with a god who cannot forgive? Is there not something wrong when a man is more compassionate than a god?

The gods are powerful. They are too powerful. They can do whatever they want and no one can stop them. They can demand that men obey them and inflict punishment on those who do not.

But whom must the gods obey? They are a law unto themselves, beholden to none.

I despise the gods. The punishment they inflict upon me is not justice. The gods do not care about justice. The gods only care about power. They wield their power as they see fit. A man can commit the most heinous crime and be forgiven if he finds favor with the gods. A man can commit the most benign act and find himself subjected to the most brutal punishment if he displeases a god.

Where is the justice in this?

Voices

Up the hill, the Stone and I go. Down the hill, the Stone and I go. Up the hill. Down the hill.

The cycle continues with an unfaltering rhythm.

As I wrestle with the Stone, I am aware of nothing but pain. Every muscle in my body is wracked with excruciating pain. It is a wonder I do not go mad.

But whenever I commence my descent down the hill, my pain is all but forgotten. My desires press upon me with an urgency not unlike that of the Stone.

"Meat!"

My stomach clamors to be fed.

"Water!"

My throat scratches and begs.

"Rest!"

My muscles plead.

"Sleep!"

My eyes insist.

Other voices speak within me, too.

My loins groan for the pleasures of a woman.

My head cries out for strong wine to dull the senses.

My heart throbs to be free of my labor with the Stone.

But these voices are suppressed by the one dominating voice that urges me on, which tells me to keep pushing despite everything.

This is the voice of fear.

I cannot cease pushing the Stone. I am afraid of what the gods might do to me. As miserable as I am, the gods can make things much worse for me. The gods can cause me such suffering that my trials with the Stone will seem insignificant in comparison. With the Stone, I know my fate.

My future is as certain as the Stone Itself.

DOUBT

Summit

I have been here, on the slope of the hill, a long time. How long, I do not know. It might be days. Or months. Or years.

It might be longer.

Time has no meaning for me. There is no past and there is no future. There is only the present.

Time moves on. Slowly. Inexorably.

I do not know if it is day or night. I do not know which season it is. I do not know if there are seasons in this forsaken place.

Everywhere I look, there is nothing but mist and murkiness. There is nothing to see. All I see is gloom.

All I feel is despair.

How high is the summit? I do not know. I cannot see more than a few steps ahead of me. I do not know if the summit is within reach or beyond reach.

I count each step. At the bottom of the hill, I begin.

One.

The Stone bears down on me with incredible force.

Two.

My shoulder is breaking under the strain. My hands and feet are torn and bleeding.

Three.

My face is pressed against the Stone. My neck is bent and ready to snap like a twig.

Four.

I catch my breath. I must rest. My arms and legs are weary and I have scarcely begun. It is always the same. I can only do so much.

The Stone does not rest. It continues to bear down upon me with Its formidable weight. I look up. I cannot see what lays ahead.

Five.

What if there is no summit? What if there is no end to this hill? What if it goes on and on and on? What if the punishment of the gods is to endlessly push the Stone with no summit to reach?

Six.

This cannot be. As surely as there is a hill, there must be a summit!

Just as the gods exist, so too must the summit exist!

Faith

I lose count.

A step forward, two steps backward. Two steps forward, a step backwards. And so it goes.

With my chest pounding hard, with my breathing furiously laboring under the strain, with every bit of my strength pushed to the limit, I cannot count my steps.

I may never know how many steps it takes to reach the summit. I may never know how far I have gone and how far I must go.

I only know that I cannot continue. The Stone

overwhelms me. Down, down It rolls, bouncing and careening along the way.

On the slope of the hill, I gaze up at a summit I cannot see. I gaze up at a sky that is shrouded in shades of gray.

I have never seen the gods. No man ever sees the gods. How can I be so certain that the gods exist?

I see the Stone and I know It exists. I can touch It and smell It. I can hear It as It bounces recklessly down the hill. My tongue licks It and It tastes of earth and dust.

The Stone is real. Are the gods real?

I wonder. Perhaps the gods do not exist. Perhaps they never existed, except in my imagination. All along, I thought that the gods have deserted me. But perhaps they were never here to begin with.

If there are no gods, why do I push the Stone? Without gods, there is no reason to push the Stone. Without gods, there is no reason to reach the summit of the hill.

There must be gods! I need the gods because there must be a reason why I push the Stone. I need the gods because there must be a reason why I strive relentlessly to reach the summit of the hill.

As surely as the Stone exists, so too must the gods exist!

Doubt

I descend the hill.

My doubts grow. What if I am wrong? What if the gods truly do not exist?

Then pushing the Stone is not a punishment.

But if pushing the Stone is not a punishment, then what is it?

There must be a reason why I continue to toil in this oppressive heat on the side of the hill with the Stone.

Was it a reason I gave to myself long ago?

As time passed, did I forget what this reason might be and begin to look upon pushing the Stone as a punishment? Did I imagine there are gods to justify pushing the Stone?

What if I no longer push the Stone up the hill? What if I simply give up?

How wonderful it would be to simply let the Stone go and watch It roll helplessly down the hill without a care!

How easy it sounds!

But I hesitate. And think.

What if the silence of the gods is not evidence of their non-existence, but evidence of their existence?

A god does not reveal himself to a man. A god conceals itself in many ways and leaves it up to a man to accept or not accept its presence. We do not see the gods because we are not meant to see them.

The gods do not speak to us because we are not

meant to hear them.

We are meant to feel them with our hearts.

My mind tells me there are no gods. My heart tells me there must be gods.

Which is it?

I yield to my uncertainty and fear. I will continue to push the Stone. As difficult as this task is, my fate in pushing the Stone is certain. To not push the Stone is to face an uncertain fate.

I cannot so easily give up that which I know and can endure, no matter how difficult and painful it may be, for an uncertain fate.

Pushing the Stone is my fate.

FREEDOM

Choice

I reach the bottom of the hill.

Despite my doubts, I must continue to labor on the side of the hill. I refuse to give up. I will not break the invisible chains that bind me to the Stone.

Once again, I begin to count my steps. One, two, three.

Before long, I lose count. Again. I start counting over.

One, two, three.

The ascent resumes. The insects continue to swarm and feast upon my flesh. The buzzing in my ears is loud and incessant. The itching is intolerable. I do not know which is worse, the brutal force of the Stone ever pushing down upon me or the ceaseless attack of the multitude of pests that find a source of food and drink in my withering body.

I do not know how far up the hill I have pushed the Stone. I do not know which is closer, the summit of the hill or the bottom of the hill. My mind is as dark and clouded as my surroundings. If only the persistent gloom that engulfs me without end would dissipate and allow me even the slightest glimpse of the world I am in!

But this is not to be. Instead, I struggle like a blind man, seeing nothing and finding my way only by the touch of my hands and feet.

How much further? Oh, why cannot I determine where my destination lay? Up there is the summit. But where up there? How far to go? I need to know! I need to know whether I can ever reach the summit with this insufferable Stone I detest so!

My strength is almost gone. I cannot continue. Though I summon every last drop of strength from muscle and sinew, I falter. It is too late. There is nothing left in me.

I let go of the Stone.

It rolls and bounces haphazardly down the hill. As I watch It bump and bobble Its way to the ground, I gaze upon It in wonder.

Why, the Stone almost seems joyous in Its chaotic descent to the bottom of the hill!

For a moment, I feel envy.

The moment passes.

As the Stone disappears into the misty gloom, I trudge down the slope and my doubts return.

I have been blaming the gods for my troubles. But what if I have only myself to blame? Do I not have a will that is free? Do I not have the power to decide my fate? What if the choice is mine whether to push the Stone?

What if it has always been my choice?

Reason

I look down.

Down there, at the base of the hill, is the Stone.

I look up.

Somewhere up there, hidden in the clouds, is the summit.

I wonder still.

Is it not my choice to push or not push the Stone?

I am not bound to this Stone with chains. Why have I surrendered my free will to gods I cannot see or hear?

I reach the bottom of the hill. I begin pushing the Stone.

A man does something more than once and it becomes a habit. Over time, a man begins to justify his habit.

I tell myself that the gods condemned me to pushing the Stone. The gods saw fit to punish me. This is what I must do.

Together, the Stone and I commence the climb anew.

Up the hill, I go. Up the hill, the Stone goes with me.

Everywhere darkness presses in on me, much like the Stone pushing down on me.

Maybe there is more to see. Maybe if I freed myself from the weight of the Stone, somewhere in the distance there is life other than my own.

The doubts in my head grow larger. They grow

so large that they overshadow the Stone.

There is a struggle within me, a struggle between head and heart. My head yearns to be free. My heart recoils and trembles with fear. I cannot bear it any longer. I cannot go on like this.

My head cries out.

"Come to your senses! Listen to reason! The choice is yours alone! You have a will that is free! Be a man!"

My heart cries out.

"Do not listen to your head! Do not give up! Do not disobey the gods! Your doubts are not real! Only the Stone is real!"

The conflict between head and heart is unbearable. They pull at one another like a taut rope on the verge of snapping.

My head prevails. I do the unthinkable.

On the slope of the hill, I deliberately release

the Stone.

I watch It roll rambunctiously down the hill, just as I have watched It so many times before.

Only this time is not like before.

I do not feel despair. I do not feel a loss of hope. I do not feel a crushing weight upon my spirit.

As the Stone settles at the base of the hill, I feel a wonderful lightness in my being.

Silence

I descend the hill. The Stone is there. It waits for me.

I gaze upon It with contempt. Without me, the Stone is powerless. It cannot move. It cannot exert Itself against me. It cannot endeavor to crush me into the ground. It cannot overwhelm my strength until I lay exhausted and unable to exert myself any longer. It does not possess the intelligence I had imparted to it. It just lays there, a solid mass of stone, without thought, without feeling, without power.

Why, the Stone is nothing without me! It

cannot ascend the hill. It cannot roll down the hill unless I am there to push It up the hill. It cannot choose to do anything. It cannot do anything unless I am there to help.

I cry out to the Stone.

"Look at you! You are weak and pathetic! You have no power over me! You have no power at all. You just sit there, a dumb piece of stone and earth and dust! You cannot speak! You cannot feel! You cannot know pain and suffering as I do! You can do nothing! You can do nothing at all except stay where you are! Without me, you are nothing!"

I look up at the heavens and cry out furiously to the gods I cannot see.

"Hear me! No longer will I sweat and toil with the Stone! No longer will I bear the burden of Its imponderable weight! No longer will I aspire to push the Stone to the summit of the hill! I am a man! I am free to make my own choices! I am free to decide my own fate! Hear my words and do what you may!"

I shake my fist defiantly. I wait for the gods to inflict their wrath upon me. I do not care. Let them do their worst and be done with it.

As always, the gods are silent.

Nothingness

I rest.

At the base of the hill, I stretch out and do nothing. The aching in my muscles subsides. My limbs feel new vigor. My mind is at ease.

The Stone is by my side. Silent. As always.

It does not move. It will never move unless I push It. I will not push It. I choose not to push It.

I lie here for a long time, doing nothing, thinking nothing. How comfortable it is!

Eventually, I sleep. I do not dream.

I awaken.

Nothing has changed. The Stone is still here, unmoving. The hill is here, towering above me. Mist and murkiness continue to surround me. My thoughts are as dismal as my surroundings.

I do not know if there are others in this desolate land. I see no one. I hear no one. I call out but there is no response.

There must be others. Somewhere. I cannot imagine a world in which I alone exist. What a bleak world that would be! A man needs companionship. A man needs others.

I want to explore. Maybe somewhere out there, beyond this veil of darkness and gloom, is a land of great beauty. A land of rolling green hills and open pastures. A land of sunlit blue seas with white-capped waves.

A land where a woman with eyes as black as sapphires waits for me.

I rise to my feet.

Free from the weight of the Stone, I feel a nimbleness in my step. With each step I take, I feel a burgeoning cheerfulness.

I set out on a journey to explore the unknown. I leave the Stone and hill behind. The Stone and the hill are my past.

My future lies ahead.

I travel across a great expanse of empty land. For how long, I do not know. Everywhere I go, there is nothing to see.

There is no land of great beauty.

There are no green fields or blue seas.

There are no animals. There are no birds.

There is no beautiful woman waiting for me.

There is nothing except a vast emptiness eating away at my soul.

I grow tired. Though I no longer push the

Stone, my spirit is weary.

I close my eyes.

I think back upon the days when I pushed the Stone. I think of the hardship I endured. The struggle was futile. What foolishness it was to think that I could ever reach the summit with the Stone!

I do not move. I do not see the point of moving. I do not see the point of doing anything at all.

After a while, I cease thinking about anything at all. I no longer think.

I only breathe.

I am vaguely conscious of the rhythm of my breathing. In and out. In and out.

But that is all.

I think nothing. I do nothing.

I open my eyes now and then, but a great

tiredness draws me back into a state of nothingness. I do not know how much time has passed. I have no sense of time. I do not know who I am or why I am here.

Whatever I am, I am no longer.

JOY

Awakening

Something stirs. Out of nothingness, there is something. I cannot describe what it is. I have no words. I have no feelings. There is no "I."

Slowly, the darkness recedes. There is a light. It is a dim light. It is at the end of a long, dark tunnel. I am drawn to this light. Either I approach it or it approaches me. I am not sure which.

The light becomes brighter. Gradually, there is an awakening of forces within me. Suddenly, there is a burst of radiance as my senses come alive.

Before me, a desolate scene appears.

There is a Stone. It is a great Stone. It rests at the base of a large hill. There is nothing else to see. There is no life other than my own.

I begin to push the Stone up the hill. I do not know why. I simply do.

Far above is the summit. It is shrouded in mist and uncertainty. With shoulder and hands against the Stone, I strain to move It. For what purpose, I do not know.

I only know that I must.

The weight of the Stone is great. It is more than I can bear. I cannot push the Stone further. It overwhelms me, pressing upon me and pulverizing me into submission. I succumb to Its immense weight. I watch helplessly as It rolls smoothly and painlessly down the hill.

I descend the hill and begin pushing It up the hill again.

I hear a voice. It is a small voice. I can hardly hear it. It is speaking to me.

What is it saying?

I do not know. I know only the Stone. Its heaviness is crushing me. Fear swells up in me. I fear the Stone will roll over me and flatten me like a bug.

I hear the voice again. It is a little louder. It is telling me something.

What is it telling me?

The voice grows louder still. Now it is shouting. It is telling me to wake up.

Wake up. Wake up.

I yield to its insistent urging.

I wake up.

Alone

I am on my back, staring up at the grayness above.

I must have been dreaming.

I remain where I am. On the ground, without moving.

How long have I been on the ground thinking nothing, feeling nothing, aware of nothing, I cannot say. It may have been moments. It may have been days. It may have been years.

Fragmented memories come to me. Memories of my struggle with the Stone. I know that many times I tried to push the Stone to the summit of the hill and many times I failed.

Or was it all a dream?

I endeavor to rise. I have no strength in my legs. Or my arms. All my strength is gone. My muscles are too weak. Too long have I lain on the ground.

I collapse.

Again, I strive to rise. I collapse to the ground once more. The process repeats itself. My frustration mounts.

Must I remain here? Must I forever grovel on the ground like a four-legged animal? Am I not a man? What does it take to stand on my two legs like a man is meant to stand?

It takes many attempts, but finally I am standing.

Everywhere I look, there is nothing to see.

There is no Stone.

There is no hill.

There is nothing.

Even the insects are gone.

I have never felt so alone.

I cannot think clearly. I need something to see. To touch and taste and smell. To hear. With nothing outside of me, I am trapped in my mind. I will go mad.

I *am* going mad.

The Stone. I must find the Stone. And the hill.

I know they were not a dream. They are out there, somewhere in the perpetual grayness of my surroundings.

I must find them both. I cannot remain alone.

I go back the way I came. It is a long trek. I wonder if I am truly walking or if it is just my imagination. There is nothing to guide me. Only emptiness.

I reach the hill. The Stone is there.

I am no longer alone.

Conflict

Shoulder to Stone, I push. My heart tells me this is what I must do.

But I hear a voice of discontent. And disagreement. My head tells me to quit. My head tells me that there is no reason to push the Stone. My head tells me that there is no reason to reach the summit of the hill. It is simply enough to know that the Stone is here and so is the hill. The flies and mosquitoes and gnats have likewise returned. I am not alone.

And yet my heart compels me otherwise.

My heart cries out, "You must push the Stone!

Do it! Do it now!"

I do nothing.

With my back to the Stone, with my feet digging into the hard ground, I pause and close my eyes and brace myself as the Stone pushes down upon me.

Why does my head keep telling me to cease this futile labor? Why does my heart tell me otherwise?

Must I forever endure this conflict between head and heart?

I take a deep breath and open my eyes.

My heart is stronger than my head. I heed the calling of my heart and ignore what my head tells me.

Up the hill, I go.

Up, up, up to a summit I know not if I can reach.

I do not give up. I cannot give up. With each

step, my will to succeed grows stronger.

I will not surrender. I will not give in to the relentless ramblings of my head, say what it will.

I keep pushing.

Being

The days pass.

The mist and gloom are gone. It is as if a veil has been lifted from my eyes.

I see the hill reaching up to touch the sky. I cannot see the summit. It is so far above that it is lost in the brilliance of the sky.

Why have I not seen this before?

I gaze at my hands. They are weathered and beaten and torn. They do not look like hands. They look like the paws of some afflicted animal.

I stare at my feet. They are as black as ancient coal. They are as ugly as feet can be.

Is this what I have become? Some misshapen vestige of a man? Is there nothing human about me that remains?

No. I am more than my body. My head tells me that I am what I think. My heart tells me that I am what I feel. My spirit tells me that I am what I dream and aspire to be and hope for.

My eyes are truly open now. There is light and color everywhere. What I see has always been here. What I once perceived as darkness was only my despair.

I gaze upon the Stone thoughtfully.

I suddenly understand what I did not understand before.

Without the Stone, I am nothing.

To give up the struggle is not to be. To do is to be.

I *am.*

Purpose

Up the hill I go.

Sweat pours unendingly down my bearded face. My wretched body drips with sweat. My blistered toes painfully dig into the hard ground. My twisted shoulder aches under the unforgiving heaviness of the Stone.

The flies are everywhere. A swarm of gnats engulfs me. They drink from my body and bite my flesh. So, too, do the other wretched insects that continually torment me.

Nothing has changed and everything has changed.

What is outside of me is as it always has been. What is within me is different from what it was.

I strain. I grunt. I push.

The Stone does not yield. The Stone seems stronger than ever. I do not give up. I do not yield.

The Stone moves. Slowly. Step by step.

The summit is far ahead, but I do not know how far. I know only that to be I must continue to struggle. I must continue to be.

The effort is more than I can bear. My spirit wanes. With each step I take, my head clamors with questions.

"Is it enough simply to be? Must there not be something more to pushing the Stone? Must there not be a purpose?"

My heart is silent. My spirit is too weak to resist.

I look up to the sky. I cry out to the gods.

"Why must I push this Stone to the summit of the hill? What is the purpose? There must be a purpose!"

The gods do not answer.

My head continues to argue.

"If there is no purpose, why continue to struggle? Why not give up the struggle and simply cease to be?"

Neither heart nor spirit reply. My head rants on.

"It is folly to push the Stone. It is folly to suffer without end. Give up and be done!"

How soundly my head argues. Its reasoning is irrefutable. Why endure the unendurable merely to know *I am*?

I acquiesce. I let go of the Stone and watch numbly as It plummets to the bottom of the hill.

My head exults in victory. My spirit is

exhausted.

Chance

Down the hill I go.

I reach the bottom of the hill. The Stone is here. Silent. Unmoving. It does not care whether I push It or not. It is merely a stone.

I sit. I rest. I do not think.

I turn my gaze upwards. Up there is the summit. It is unreachable.

I stare at the sky. How beautiful the sky looks. It is like a beautiful sea, much like the beautiful sea of my dreams.

I do not move. I sit and gaze at the sky until the sun sets.

I watch the night sky in awe as the moon and stars appear.

I have never seen the moon and stars before, except in my dreams. It is a beautiful sight to behold.

Still, I do not move.

The sun rises. The sun sets. The cycle continues, day after day, night after night.

I watch the moon as it appears in its phases. I watch the motions of the stars in the heavens. The motions of the celestial bodies bespeak nothing of gods. If there are gods, their silence is stifling.

Day after day, night after night, I sit and watch the sun and the moon and the stars.

It is a mesmerizing sight.

As time passes, I begin to see a natural order to the universe. The sun rises and sets because it obeys natural laws. The moon appears in its phases not because of the gods, but because of the laws of nature. The world and everything in it are a part of this natural order.

I now see a universe set in motion by laws I do not understand. It is a universe without gods. A universe without gods is a cold, unfeeling universe. It is a universe that takes no account of a man's actions and judges them right or wrong. It is a universe in which a man is at the mercy of the crude, indiscriminating forces of nature. Perhaps nothing in this universe is by design, and everything is by chance. Perhaps the universe is an accident.

Am I nothing more than an accident in an accidental universe?

Dawn

The sun rises.

Many days and nights have passed and I have not moved. An old lethargy has set upon me and once again the forces of inaction and sluggishness draw me downward. I have no desire to move, no desire to do anything.

As the early morning light falls upon my face, I open my eyes. I am in a daze, not knowing where I am or who I am.

Slowly, I awaken from my stupor and my head begins to clear.

Above the horizon, the rising sun is a huge

reddish orb of marvelous beauty. It is more beautiful than I thought possible, than I ever imagined possible. I sit in awe of the new dawn.

What a wondrous sight to behold! Why have I not seen before the beauty in this magnificent act of nature?

I rest next to the Stone with outstretched legs and let my entire being soak in the majesty of the sunrise. I do not move nor do I wish to move. I want nothing more than to absorb the sublime beauty of what I see.

Overwhelmed with emotion, I reach over and touch the Stone, my only companion in this forsaken place, and gently stroke It. I do not know why. What I see is an experience I wish to share. It is an experience that deserves to be shared with someone very close, like a lover or a cherished friend.

I glance over at the Stone. Does It feel as I do? Does It feel like I do that we are not just witnesses to this awe-inspiring event, but we are a necessary part of it? Where is beauty unless there is someone to behold it?

Resting my head against the Stone, I feel enlivened by Its presence.

Together, we watch the sunrise, head to Stone, Stone to head.

Friend

As I watch the sun rise above the horizon, an idea dawns on me.

Something in the universe struggles just as I do. I know not what this might be, but it brings order to chaos, sets the sun and moon and stars in motion, and keeps them there.

I lower my head and turn to look at the Stone. I speak to It.

“Perhaps the universe is no different than you and me. Perhaps the universe struggles to know itself. Maybe it needs us to become aware. If there are gods, perhaps they struggle as do we. They may each have their own hill to climb, their own Stone to push."

I rest my eyes upon the Stone in quiet appreciation. Bathed in the splendid golden rays of the morning sun, It does not appear so intimidating. There is a subdued charm to It. I have never seen the Stone in this light before. It is as if I am seeing It for the first time

A smile creases my face. I do not remember the last time I smiled.

I gaze up at the sky. Not at the sun, which hovers not far above the horizon, but much higher. Higher than the summit of the hill – up to the apex of the sky.

Filled with awe, words thoughtfully issue from my parched lips.

"Maybe pushing the Stone was never a punishment, but a gift."

Overcome with emotion, I lower my gaze once again and set it upon the Stone.

"Not to take up the struggle is to be not a man, but a stone. If I do nothing, I am no better than this Stone."

I rest my head against the Stone. I tell myself that the Stone is my ally and not my foe. Whereas before I saw the Stone as an enemy to be reviled, I now see It as a friend to be revered. And I see that this hill is not my perdition.

It is my garden.

Joy

The Stone awaits.

I rise. I lay my hands upon It, not with contempt but with respect. And love.

We begin the struggle anew. In this struggle to reach the summit, I see my place in the universe. I am not alone here. All that is in the universe is with me.

Here, on the slope of the hill, the Stone crushes me. It pushes me to the earth. I do not cast blame upon It. We are not so different, each stubborn in our resolve.

Under the oppressive weight of the Stone, I am

filled with doubt and dread. When I am able to struggle no longer and must give up, all hope is destroyed. But when the weight of the Stone is lifted from my shoulder and I descend the hill, hope arises anew. I feel reborn.

Pushing the Stone is what I am supposed to do. I feel it. I feel it in my bones.

Up the hill, down the hill. I move in rhythm with the universe.

I am filled with new resolve. If I reach the summit, does it matter? I do not know. I do not know what awaits me up there, somewhere in the vast blue sky above. I do not know what I will become. It matters only that I take up the struggle.

I see now that happiness is not to be found in the attainment of the summit. Happiness is found in the struggle to attain the summit.

On the slope of the hill, I stand my ground and

reach for the stars. The summit awaits. Up there.

I belong here. In this struggle, I know who I am. In this struggle, I know my place in the universe. In this struggle, there is hope when reason tells me there should be none. Reason tells me it is a futile task, but do I really know? I only know that I am. That is enough.

My spirit soars. I raise my fist in triumph.

Who am I?

On the slope of the hill, under the weight of the Stone, I shed tears. They are tears of joy.

I am Sisyphus!